SLIP STREAM

WALK INTO
DANGER

DAVID AND HELEN ORME
Illustrated by KEVIN HOPGOOD

LONDON BOROUGH OF BARNET
LIBRARY SERVICES
WITHDRAWN AND OFFERED
FOR SALE
SOLD AS SEEN

PRICE

30131 05046526 6

LONDON BOROUGH OF BARNET

D0928505

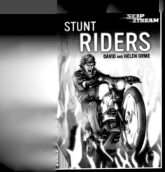

STUNT RIDERS
DAVID and HELEN ORME

978 1 4451 1314 2 pb

UNARMED AND DANGEROUS
DAVID and HELEN ORME

978 1 4451 1316 6 pb

WALK INTO DANGER
DAVID and HELEN ORME

978 1 4451 1318 0 pb

...hic fiction

ALIEN CAGE
JONNY ZUCKER and SIKU

978 1 4451 1322 7 pb

FUTURE TENSE
JONNY ZUCKER and LEE CARTER

978 1 4451 1320 3 pb

THE DECIDERS
JONNY ZUCKER and ANDREW CHIU

978 1 4451 1324 1 pb

...-fiction

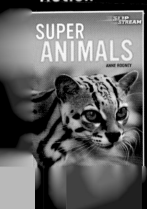

SUPER ANIMALS
ANNE ROONEY

GREATEST ROCK BANDS
ANNE ROONEY

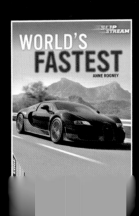

WORLD'S FASTEST
ANNE ROONEY

SLIP STREAM

WALK INTO
DANGER

DAVID AND **HELEN ORME**
Illustrated by **KEVIN HOPGOOD**

EDGE FRANKLIN WATTS

LONDON·SYDNEY

First published in 2012 by
Franklin Watts
338 Euston Road
London NW1 3BH

Franklin Watts Australia
Level 17/207 Kent Street
Sydney NSW 2000

Text © David and Helen Orme 2012
Illustration © Franklin Watts 2012

The rights of David and Helen Orme to be
identified as the authors and Kevin Hopgood
as the illustrator of this Work have been
asserted in accordance with the Copyright,
Designs and Patents Act, 1988.

All rights reserved

A CIP catalogue record for this book is
available from the British Library.

ISBN 978 1 4451 1318 0

Series Editors: Adrian Cole and Jackie Hamley
Series Advisors: Diana Bentley and Dee Reid
Series Designer: Peter Scoulding

1 3 5 7 9 10 8 6 4 2

Printed in China

Franklin Watts is a division of
Hachette Children's Books,
an Hachette UK company.
www.hachette.co.uk

CONTENTS

CHAPTER 1
LOST!

Simon and Lia were on a hike.

They were using a map to find their way.

"I think we're lost," said Lia. "We must

be reading the map wrong."

Then Simon skidded on some loose stones and slipped over. His phone fell out of his pocket and went over some rocks.

CHAPTER 2
SNOWFALL

"Things can't get much worse," said Lia.

Then it began to snow.

"Oh yes they can!" said Simon.

Soon they couldn't even see the path.

"Now we're really lost!" said Lia.

She began to panic.

"There are some steep cliffs near here.

I saw them on the map," she said.

"Listen!" said Simon.

They could hear a voice calling.

"Help! Help!"

They found a man by a steep cliff.

"Am I glad to see you!" said the man. "I'm Joe.

My bike skidded. I jumped off but it fell down

the cliff. I think I've broken my leg. Can you

call for help?"

CHAPTER 3
A CALL FOR HELP

"We've no phone," said Simon. "Can you get your phone?"

"My phone is in the pack on my bike. And my bike is at the bottom of that cliff," said Joe.

"I'll climb down and get the phone," said Lia.

The snow had made the rocks very slippery.

Lia knew if she fell she would die.

At last Lia got down to the bike.

CHAPTER 4
HELICOPTER RESCUE

Lia checked the phone. It was OK!

She called the Rescue team.

"Send a helicopter. Quickly!" she said.

Then she shone the light from the bike into the sky

so the helicopter could find them.

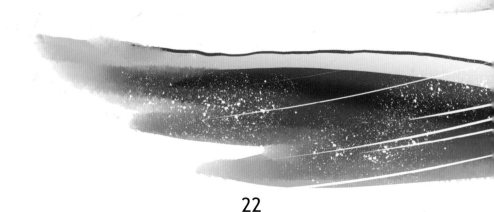

At last they heard the helicopter.

The Rescue team helped Joe and

Simon into the helicopter.

Then they dropped a rope for Lia.

"You're very lucky," one of the Rescue team
told Joe. "One more hour in this cold and
you could have died."

"Lucky for me you two are no good at reading
a map!" Joe said to Simon and Lia.

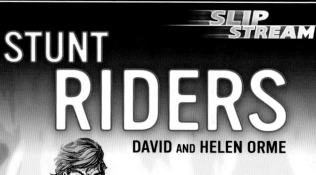

STUNT
RIDERS

DAVID AND HELEN ORME

EDGE

Zak and Jed are stunt bike riders. Dan comes
to see their show. He wants to be a stunt bike rider too.

Zak and Jed do the exploding coffin trick. Everyone cheers!
They are the best stunt riders in the world.
But what is their secret?

LONDON·SYDNEY

UNARMED AND
DANGEROUS

DAVID and HELEN ORME

CAUTION
WET FLOOR

CLEANING
IN PROGRESS

Nita wants to go out, but her dad says she has
to help in the shop. So Nita decides to have some fun!

Nita's fun leads to a big mess and her dad
is not happy. Then two robbers rush into
the shop. Can Nita stop them?

LONDON•SYDNEY

About SLIPSTREAM

Slipstream is a series of expertly levelled books designed for pupils who are struggling with reading. Its unique three-strand approach through fiction, graphic fiction and non-fiction gives pupils a rich reading experience that will accelerate their progress and close the reading gap.

At the heart of every Slipstream fiction book is a great story. Easily accessible words and phrases ensure that pupils both decode and comprehend, and the high interest stories really engage older struggling readers.

Whether you're using Slipstream Level 1 for Guided Reading or as an independent read, here are some suggestions:

1. Make each reading session successful. Talk about the text before the pupil starts reading. Introduce any unfamiliar vocabulary.

2. Encourage the pupil to talk about the book using a range of open questions. For example, what would they do in Lia's situation?

3. Discuss the differences between reading fiction, graphic fiction and non-fiction. What do they prefer?

Slipstream Level 1 photocopiable **WORKBOOK** ISBN: 978 1 4451 1609 9 available – download free sample worksheets from: www.franklinwatts.co.uk

For guidance, SLIPSTREAM Level 1– Walk Into Danger has been approximately measured to:

National Curriculum Level: 2c
Reading Age: 7.0–7.6
Book Band: Turquoise

ATOS: 1.9*
Guided Reading Level: H
Lexile® Measure (confirmed): 320L

*Please check actual Accelerated Reader™ book level and quiz availability at www.arbookfind.co.uk